For
Gabrielle
and
Francis

This book is only possible
because of my friendship
with Lorraine Slattery

The Marshmallow Ghosts
by
L.V. Chapel

Illustrated
Tara DeWorsop

Art Director
Dice Garcia

Chapel Entertainment Press
©2015

It is a cool, windy Halloween morning.
The Old Farmer Brown Ranch has been abandoned for years.
No one knows what had happened to poor old Farmer Brown.
But now a family of ghosts have made the ranch their home.

Inside, Frankie, Laurie and little Mikey are having breakfast with Aunt Esther.

Aunt Esther explains that Mommy and Daddy work during Halloween haunting other abandoned houses. They do this so that one day the children can have their own haunted homes to raise their families.

Frankie is upset though and wants to know why he can't help! Frankie feels like he is old enough to haunt houses with his Mom and Dad.

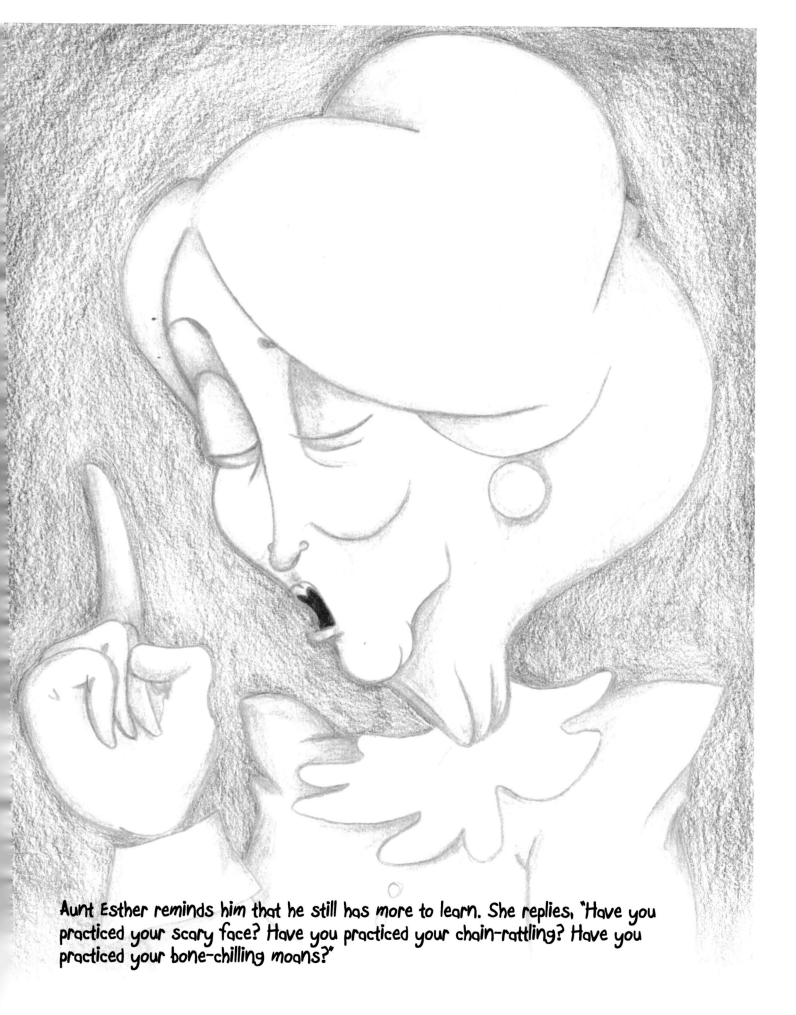

Aunt Esther reminds him that he still has more to learn. She replies, "Have you practiced your scary face? Have you practiced your chain-rattling? Have you practiced your bone-chilling moans?"

Aunt Esther brings the young ghosts to the living room and begins to tell them the tales of Halloween's past. "Years ago in places like Transylvania, Salem, and Amityville, your parents and I worked very hard to haunt houses so well, that no one dared to visit them. Because they knew they would be scared to death!"

But as time passed, our success made us ghosts lazy. And soon, people started to write books about our stories at Halloween. Then Hollywood began to make movies of those stories, turning our homes into tourist attractions. College kids would have frat parties at our homes. And younger kids would just vandalize them. Before we knew it, it got so bad we ghosts couldn't hear ourselves think. We had lost our ability to frighten people off. So we were forced to move on. And today your parents have to work even harder to secure abandoned homes at Halloween; that one day, you all can have your very own home to raise your young ones.

Later... Frankie, Laurie, and Mickey tried taking a nap in the basement. But Frankie loses his temper and shouts, "This basket isn't big enough for all three of us. I'm going downtown to prove to Aunt Esther that I can be just as scary as mom and dad."

Laurie warns him, "Mom and Dad have said NEVER to go into town without them. We don't know what could happen!"

"Nonsense, scaredy pants!" Frankie replies as he floats out the basement window, "You can stay here with Mikey or you can grab him and follow me!"

"Weeee!!! Now THAT'S what I'm talking about!", Frankie gleefully yells as the three young ghosts float over the tree tops heading for downtown.

From the sky, they can see the streets and sidewalks filled with kids trick-or-treating with their parents. They twist and twirl in the air from the excitement at having their very first outdoor Halloween!

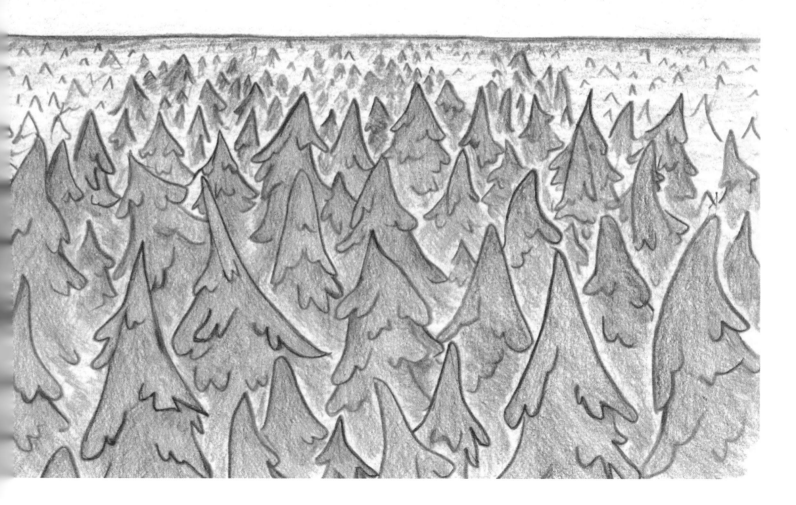

Frankie, Laurie and Mikey arrive and stop in the middle of the downtown area. They watch in amazement as kids wearing all different types of costumes walk by them. Even store owners are giving out treats to the kids.

As Laurie and Frankie watch in disbelief, Frankie asks, "Are those ghost relatives?" Laurie answers, "I don't know?"
Just then, Mikey whispers into Laurie's ear. Laurie pauses for a moment, and replies softly, "I miss mommy and daddy, too."

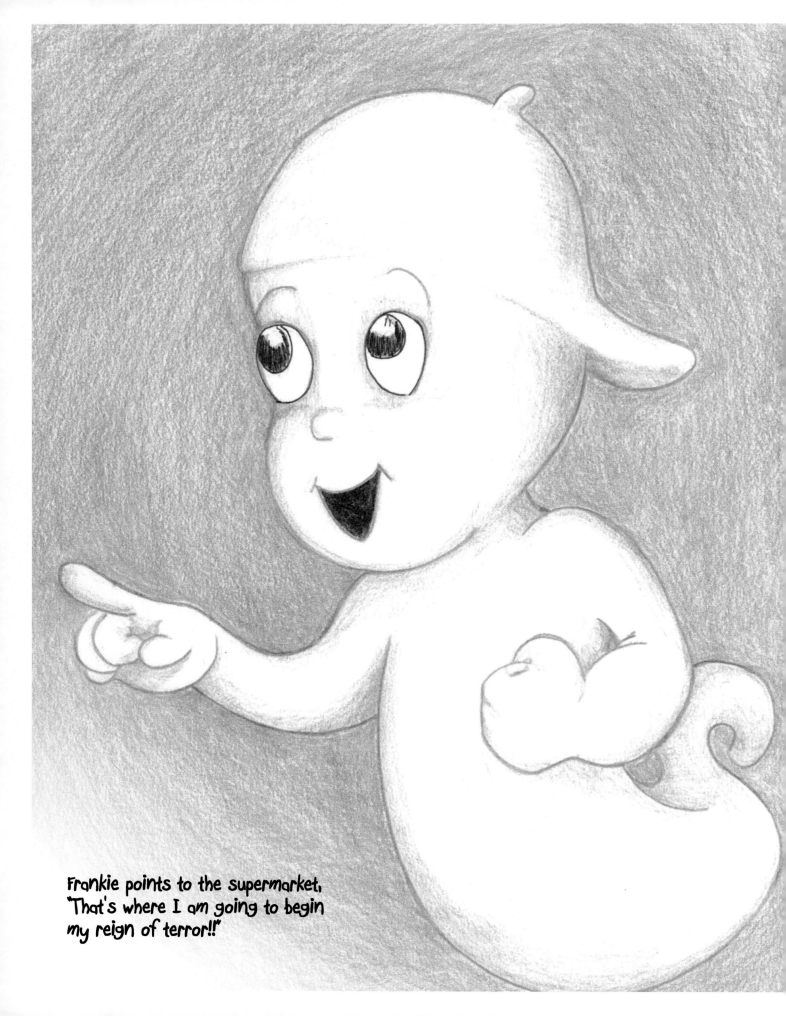

Frankie points to the supermarket,
"That's where I am going to begin
my reign of terror!!"

Laurie tries to stop him, but before she can speak another word, Frankie is floating into the supermarket followed by Mikey.

Frankie flies around the store knocking boxes off shelves and throwing canned food onto the floor. The shoppers are frightened because they don't understand what's happening!

Frankie giggles with excitement, while scaring a mother with her child.

"This is great! I told you! Did you see me scare those shoppers? Did you see me scare the deli man? Did you see me..." Suddenly Frankie and Laurie become silent. They look at one another and say, "Did you see Mikey?"

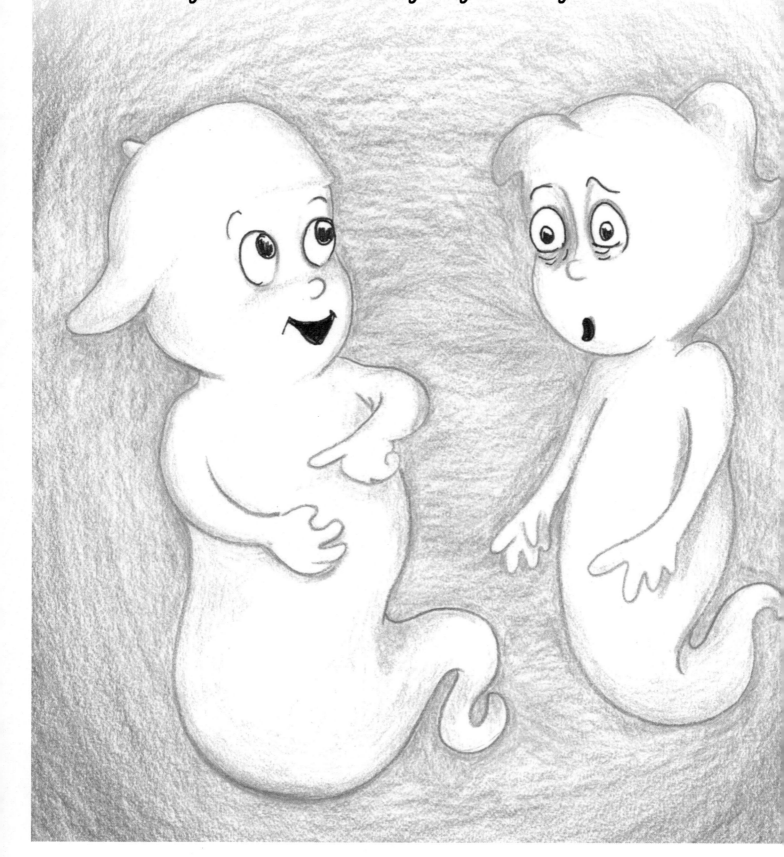

Back at the ranch, Aunt Esther is looking for the young ghosts. "Goodness gracious, where in the dickens have you children gone." Aunt Esther floats down the basement stairs thinking, "I thought I told you crafty spooks to stay here until your parents came home. I understand you may think your old enough..." Aunt Esther stops in her tracks, "Oh lord Frankie you didn't. Oh no, they didn't!" It becomes clear to Aunt Esther that the young ghosts have left the ranch and gone down town.

The supermarket manager has made a table of hot chocolate and marshmallows for the children and their parents. As the manager gives out the refreshments to the crowd gathering around the table,

Mikey has made his way to the end of the table where there is a tray of marshmallows sitting unprotected. Mikey takes one marshmallow and eats it. Mikey likes it so much, he takes a second one, then a third one, then another...

Frankie and Laurie spot Mikey. They look on in horror as Mikey gobbles down the marshmallows. As Mikey eats, something strange begins to happen. Mikey is no longer an invisible ghost! Now he can be seen by everyone in the supermarket!! Somehow the marshmallows Mikey has been eating are making him look like a little boy in a ghost costume!

The manager walks over to Mikey and says, "My dear boy, if you continue to eat these marshmallows you will certainly be sick to your stomach. Where is your mother?" Mikey mumbles with his mouth full of marshmallows. The manager doesn't understand a word and says, "You wait right here. I will call your mother over the loudspeakers."

MARSHMALLOWS

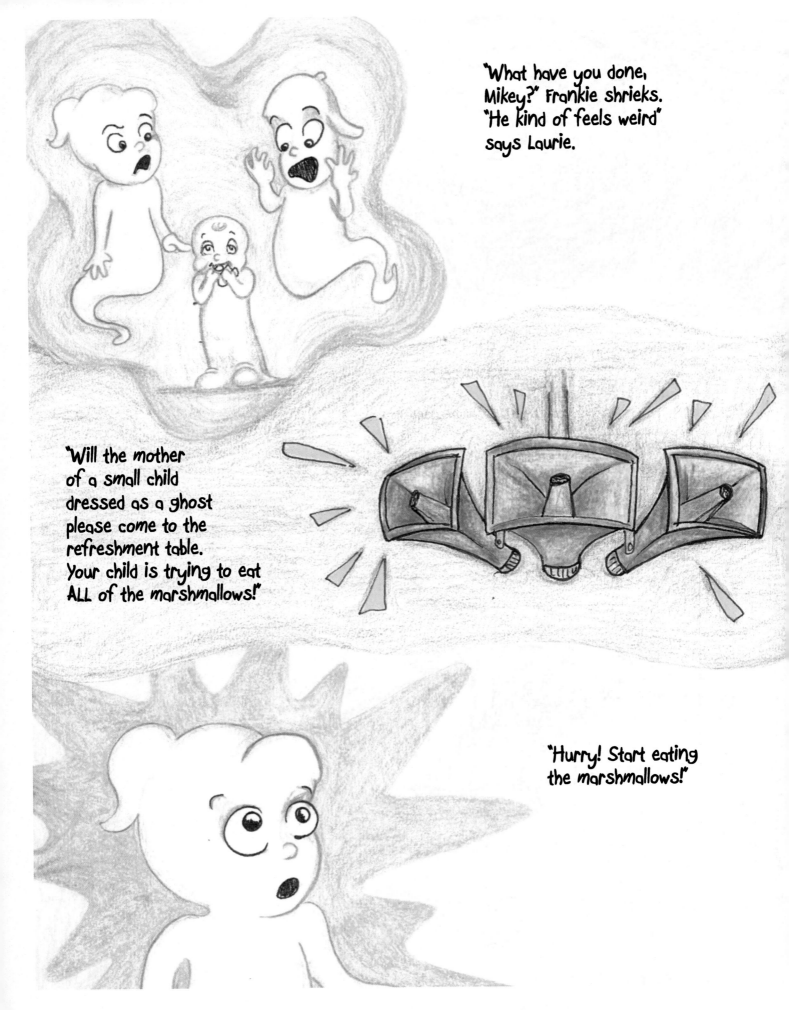

Frankie and Laurie begin eating marshmallows. Soon, like Mikey, Frankie and Laurie can be seen by everyone in the supermarket! The store manager walks back over to see all three together and says, "Hello, do you know this child?"

Laurie looks at Frankie and says, "Ahh, he's our brother." And they slowly walk out of the supermarket.

Frankie, Laurie and Mikey stand quietly in the middle of the town square. They smile as they watch all the children having fun. The mothers bring their children trick-or-treating to all the stores. Mikey mumbles something to Laurie. Laurie tells him that Mom and Dad are out working and that maybe next year they can all come back together with them.

"Nonsense!" Frankie yells, "We're here to scare people! To show Aunt Esther we can haunt houses just like Mom and Dad."

Laurie becomes a little confused. "But how can we do that if everyone can see us now?"

A lady walks over to Frankie, Laurie and Mikey
with some lollipops. "My goodness gracious!
How adorable are you three!
Are you brothers and sister?"
Frankie, Laurie and Mikey look at each other,
then the lady... and slowly nod yes.
"Well here you go, Happy Halloween!"

"Boy, this looks yummy" says Laurie

"Hey! Remember why we are here!"

Suddenly Frankie is grabbed by a young, pretty, tomboy girl named, "Gabrielle."
She asks, "Hey is that velvet or microfiber, SLEEPING FOAM!"
Frankie says nothing. "What's the matter, cat got your tongue? Where are your parents?"
Frankie answers, "working."
"So's my dad. But my mom is in heaven."

So I'm a Halloween orphan just like you. Where do you live? Gabrielle asks.

"Over by the Farmer Brown Ranch" replies Frankie.

"Whoa... I thought that place was haunted. You and your folks must be mighty brave living there."

Hey, do you want to go trick-or-treating with me?" Gabrielle asks.

Frankie turns to his brother and sister; but Laurie and Mikey have left him to play in the town square. Gabrielle asks Frankie who he is looking for, and Frankie shrugs his shoulders and replies, "Sure, let's go."

Gabrielle and Frankie walk over to the school running track.
"The girls don't like me much because I play too rough and the boys don't like me
because I'm a girl. My Dad thinks I talk too much; but I get excited when I meet
someone new. If you're hot in that costume you can take it off if you want"
Gabrielle says.

Frankie shakes his head and says, "No." "OK, I get it. You're hardcore.
The costume doesn't come off 'til' Halloween is over! That's cool." Gabrielle quips.

All of a sudden, Augie the school bully hits Gabrielle in the head with an egg! Frankie helps to wipe the egg off of Gabrielle's face.

Augie throws another egg, but this time it hits the back of Frankie's head and bounces right back at Augie hitting him in the face!

Augie becomes so angry, he lashes out at Gabrielle and Frankie. "Okay, Casper and Butch, I'm going to break all these eggs on your face!" As Augie and his buddies grab the eggs, Frankie begins to grow into a terrifying ghost and lets out a horrifying blood curdling howl.

Augie and his buddies freeze in their tracks, drop their eggs and run away like scared little mice. Frankie smiles as he watches them run, then turns to Gabrielle, but she is not there. Gabrielle was just as scared and ran away!

Frankie becomes sad knowing he scared Gabrielle too. Laurie and Mikey find Frankie. "Hey, Frankie! We didn't know where you went so Mikey and I went trick-or-treating! Look at all our stuff! Isn't this neat?" "I saw you from all the way over there and you looked a hundred feet tall! What happened?"

Frankie just bows his head and says "nothing".

Aunt Esther finds them at last. "Oh my sweet heaven there you all are, and what in the blazes happened to you three. Your parents will thrash me if they see you like this!"

But as the Sun goes down Aunt Esther watches in amazement as Frankie, Laurie and Mikey slowly turn back to regular ghosts. She watches with her mouth open, but is unable to say anything. Aunt Esther then gives them all a hug as they make their way back to the ranch.

When the four return home, Mom and Dad are waiting for them. They ask where they have all been, and Aunt Esther tells them they were in the fields playing and lost track of time. Dad sees that Frankie seems unhappy and pulls him aside to talk to him in private.

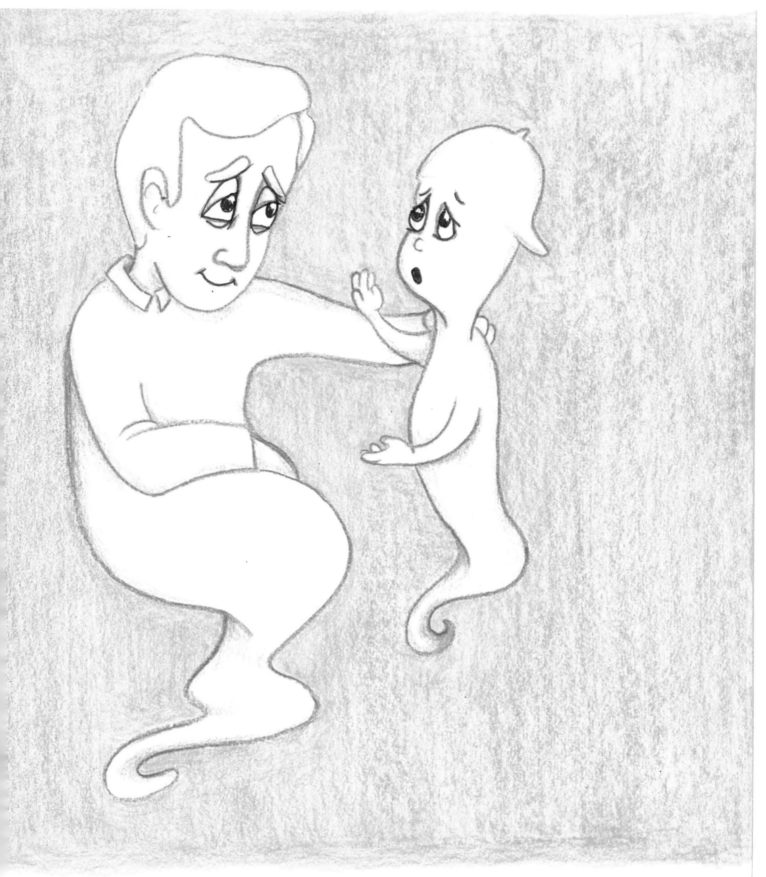

"I could tell Aunt Esther was fibbing a bit. I want you to tell me the truth, Frankie." said his Dad. Frankie tells his father everything from sneaking away, to changing to marshmallow, to scaring Gabrielle and the bullies. His Dad listens to the whole story - especially the part where Frankie felt left out of the family tradition.

Frankie's Dad thanks him for being honest and explains that sometimes parents get so caught up with all their responsibilities to their children that they forget how fast they really grow up. He hugs Frankie and apologizes then says, "I think it's time for a new Halloween tradition!"

The old Farmer Brown Ranch has gone through a complete transformation. The grounds are cleaned. The tractor is fixed. Laurie and her Mom are serving hot chocolate and marshmallows to parents and kids, who are all dressed in Halloween costumes.

Frankie stands off to the side with a big smile on his face as he watches his family, who are all now visible to the rest of the crowd after eating the marshmallows. Then suddenly, he becomes a little nervous. He sees Gabrielle and her Dad walking up the road. Frankie stands there until she reaches him.

"Hi, Frankie."

"Hi, Gabrielle."

Gabrielle's Dad sees them and says, "I'll get some hot chocolate for us."

Gabrielle thanks her Dad and then once they are alone she asks, "Am I the only who knows you and your family are real ghosts?"

Frankie replies, "Pretty much." Then Frankie tries to apologize to Gabrielle for scaring her, but she stops him.

"I realize you were trying to protect me, not trying to hurt me. That's why I came here. I also wanted to ask you a question." Frankie nods, "Sure, anything." And Gabrielle asks, "Do you ever see my Mom?" Frankie is silent for a moment then speaks, "I'm sorry Gabrielle, I'm just a ghost. But your mom... she's an Angel."

Gabrielle smiles while holding back tears. Then she and Frankie hug. Gabrielle whispers to Frankie, "Thank you."

"Hi, I'm Gabrielle's Dad. This was a cool idea. The place looks awesome. The kids are having fun." Frankie's Dad grins and says, "I can't take the credit. It was my son Frankie's idea." "He must be a good kid" said Gabrielle's Dad. But Frankie's Dad corrects him, "No, he's a great kid." "You're absolutely right... by the way, those costumes, are they velour or neoprene?"